THE CROCODILE WITH THE CROOKED SMILE

Written by Katie Wowers
& Illustrated by Graham Evans

This is a work of fiction. No crocodiles, lions, giraffes, elephants, zebras, hyenas, or hippopotamuses were harmed in the writing of this book. Imagination is the most wonderful thing. Use it and enjoy it.

First paperback edition 2021

Written by Katie Wowers
Illustrations by Graham Evans

ISBN, paperback: 978-1-80227-259-8
ISBN, ebook: 978-1-80227-260-4
ISBN, Hardback: 978-1-80227-261-1

My darling Ammy,
May you always be kind and strong in equal measure.
Be true to yourself and if you're ever in doubt,
know that I will believe in you enough for the both of us.
I love you so much.
Mummy

This story begins on the African Plain,
Where herds of thirsty animals waited desperately for rain.
In one peculiar herd were an Elephant and a Giraffe,
A Lion, a Zebra and Hyena with a cackling laugh.

"I'm thirsty!" squealed the Zebra. "I feel ever so jaded.
I'm so dehydrated, my stripes have all faded!"
"I'm shrinking!" declared the Giraffe. "My neck's getting shorter!
I'm utterly gasping; I'll do anything for water."

Then, as if by magic, when the drought was taking its toll,
They found just what they'd wished for; a great deep watering hole.
But on the surface by the water's edge and much to their surprise,
They spotted something rather strange; two squinting yellowy eyes.

The water rippled, they heard a **SPLASH**, then saw a beaming smile.
And so, they breathed a sigh of relief; just a friendly Crocodile.
Then, with the **sweetest** crooked smile, he announced,
"Welcome all, please come and drink!"
But the animals shook and shuddered, making Croc's heart truly sink.

The Elephant turned and whispered, "Let's go; he makes me quiver!"
Then flapped her ears and said out loud, "We'll find another river".
"Wait! Let's drink together," said Croc, grinning from ear to ear.
But the animals looked the other way, pretending not to hear.

Swooshing his mane, the Lion roared, "That Crocodile cramps my style!"
"I'm the King of the Jungle ... he's just a Croc with a crooked smile."
"Go away," the Hyena sniggered, glancing at Croc so smugly,
"We can't be seen with a Crocodile; you're just far too ugly."

The animals did not care ... or they seemed to be forgetting,
That Crocodiles have feelings too; their words were quite upsetting.
As Croc swam away, he muttered, "I wish I could disappear".
That evening, sad and all alone, he shed a little tear.

"Am I really so ugly?" he thought. "Should I wear a disguise?"
He swam on blindly, his vision was blurred, due to the tears in his eyes.
Feeling blue and lonely, Croc sniffled; his throat had a lump,
Then suddenly, in the murky water, his nose crumpled up with a **BUMP!**

It'll stop you feeling down, and you won't be gloomy or glum,
If, like our Croc, you find yourself bumping into a hippo's bum!
"Who's that?" honked the Hippo. "You just made me panic.
I feel like the iceberg hit by the Titanic!"

"I'm sorry!" said Croc. "Did I give you a scare?
I didn't mean to collide with your derrière."
"Don't worry," grinned Hippo, "you did make me jump,
But my bottom's well-cushioned; it's perfectly plump!"

"You're not cross?" asked Croc. "You're proud of your behind?
I swam into your buttocks and you really don't mind?"

"No, no," said Hippo. "I don't want to tussle.
I'm sure you'll agree, this rump is pure muscle."

With a wink, Hippo declared, "I'd like to be your friend!
I think it must be fate that you crashed into my rear end."

"Me too!" Croc agreed. "And could I have some advice,
About these other animals, who weren't very nice?"

"They said hurtful things and it made me unhappy.
My lips are now twitching and I'm feeling quite snappy...
They were mean!" he grumbled. "They're not a nice gang."
Croc's mouth began to water, then came a hunger pang.

"You're majestic," said Hippo. "Crocs are perfectly evolved!
Just ignore them, my friend... relax, problem solved!"
But Croc felt confused; he had a strange urge to defeat them.
"I've got it!" he declared. "It's very simple. I'll EAT them!"

"You're joking!" laughed Hippo. "You're being sarcastic.
You can't eat them, dear Croc. That's really quite drastic."
"But now I'm hangry*!" said Croc. "They're a bullying bunch.
Yes, I'll gobble them up for a scrumptious lunch."

*bad-tempered or irritable as a result of hunger

Whilst hatching a plan to use his famous death-roll,
He licked his lips and thought … "Perhaps I'll eat them whole?
To start, before my main, I will nibble on neck of Giraffe.
When they see what Crocs can do, they won't tease or laugh!"

SPECIALS

Pan fried neck of
Giraffe

Loin of Lion wrapped
Elephant ears

Fillet of Zebra with
roasted Hyena tail

All dishes will be
served with a side
of Elephant trunk.

"Main course will be loin of Lion, with a side of Elephant trunk.
Then great big ears ... then great big ribs ... then belly, a great big hunk!
I'll finish my meal with a lighter bite, tender meat, a little leaner.
I'll munch on a Zebra fillet, alongside the tail of Hyena."

"Off our Crocodile swam, determined that he would find,
Those cold-hearted, foolish animals, who'd been so very unkind.
And after his fine safari feast, Croc returned to wait ...
By the water's edge, for new friends to come, who'd have a much nicer fate.

Spotting a herd across the Plains, he rejoiced, "It's the great migration!
The wildebeest are coming for some much-needed hydration."
Bursting with excitement, "New friends!" he merrily did think.
And with the **sweetest** crooked smile, Croc announced,
"Welcome all, please come and drink!"

If there's one thing to remember ... and to learn from this short book.
Be kind to other people; don't judge them for how they look.
Be gracious, fair and thoughtful. Consider how they feel.
And most of all, be thankful that you're not our Croc's next meal!

Printed in Great Britain
by Amazon